Developing Henry

Mari Sexton

Easy to read. Hard to put down.
A Storyshares book — storyshares.org

Published by Storyshares, LLC.

The characters and events in this book are fictitious.
Any similarity to real persons, living
or dead, is entirely coincidental.

Storyshares, LLC
24 N. Bryn Mawr Avenue, #340
Bryn Mawr, PA 19010-3304
www.storyshares.org

Inspiring reading with a new kind of book.

Interest level: High School
Grade Level Equivalent: 1.8

ISBN 9798885977524

Printed in the United States.

Book design by Storyshares, LLC

Developing Henry

Mari Sexton

Chapter 1

"You can't be that stupid!" my brother, Hector, yells at me.

In an instant, my mom is there, yelling at him. "We do not use the word 'stupid' in our house."

My brother looks at the floor and then at me. He reaches out to hit my shoulder, then says, "Let me help you with that."

I stand there, not knowing exactly what had happened, but feeling it was a bad thing.

I look at my mother, who has balled up her hands into fists. My brother looks like he has been kicked, hard.

All I can say is, "It's cool, bro."

Together, my brother and I go into the kitchen. He explains that the peanut butter is in the cabinet and the jelly and bread are in the refrigerator.

"Why aren't they all in the same place?" I ask.

I see his chest rise and hear him breathe in and out.

I think, "He feels like me; he doesn't know the right answer."

Then he says, "I don't know, that's just where

Mom puts them."

It makes me happy to hear Hector say he doesn't know. There are a bunch of things I don't know.

Chapter 2

Learning where the peanut butter, jelly, and bread are is no biggie.

There are things I really want to learn. But I just can't figure out how I am going to learn them.

I cannot ask my mom. There are just some things a boy does not ask his mom.

Besides, I'm sure she wouldn't be able to answer my questions.

I could ask my dad . . . but he won't be home for another three weeks. He's a truck driver for Swift and he's traveling for a while.

I could ask my sister . . . She always takes time to sit and talk to me. She is very good at explaining things I don't understand.

When I was little, she would make me sing a song for everything I did so I could remember how to do it.

I still sing the one to brush my teeth. It says, "I got my toothpaste, I got my brush, my teeth are clean, when I brush, I will have a happy smile."

Well, I'm not sure if those are all the words, but those are the words I remember and sing.

It's not what I should be singing as a freshman in high school, but it has always stuck in my head. And it reminds me of my sister.

I just don't know about asking her the questions I have. She's older and has been out of high school for a while.

I'm not sure that she will remember what it is like to be my age.

The one I should ask is Hector. He would know.

He's two or three years older than me. He'd remember what it's like.

I just don't know if I want to ask him. He gets so mad at me all the time for not knowing stuff.

I'll just wait. I don't need to do anything yet.

I make myself a peanut butter and jelly sandwich, sit in front of the tv, and veg.

I won't make anyone mad this way.

Chapter 3

It is time to go. We're going across the line to help set up for a party that will start later tonight. It is my *tío's* anniversary.

I don't like crossing the border. I hate waiting in line to get there and come back. But here we go.

I sit in the back seat listening to music. I get a text.

wau^2

I answer *NMU.*

wtho

cn't 2day

I get tired of listening to music. I play a game. I get tired of that, too.

I put my head back and stare at the car roof.

Chapter 4

We finally cross the border. We drive to the edge of the city to the hall where the party is going to be.

It's a bumpy ride. There are holes in the road.

We finally get there and a cloud of dust covers us as we park. We wait for the dust to go over us, then get out of the car.

We walk into the hall. Our *tíos* and our cousins are there.

Thomas and Angelica walk over to us. The three of us head outside while the adults stay inside.

We are looking toward the border. We can see the wall that President Trump started.

It looks like a long line of sticks from the hall. I can't see anything on the other side of it. On this side of it, there is a dirt road and weeds.

Thomas says we should get closer to it and see what happens when we do.

Angelica doesn't want to do that. She is afraid of the border patrol.

I don't want to do it either. But I don't say anything. I don't want Thomas to think I'm scared.

Chapter 5

Our *tíos* and Mom come out of the hall. "Come help us get this stuff out of the cars!" they say.

We walk over. They give us each a box. We're supposed to put it on the floor in the hall and come back for more.

We make about three trips before we have everything unloaded. Then it's time for a break.

We all go to the kitchen and are told where to find cold drinks. There are cold sodas and beer. There are also bottles of wine and whiskey. Maybe it is tequila. I don't know.

I don't know much about drinking. That's something I want to know about, too.

Who would I talk to about that? Not my brother, that is for sure.

Maybe I should talk to Thomas. He's a freshman, too.

Chapter 6

We don't even get to finish our drinks because *Tío* Beto, another *tío*, walks in and says, "Help me move the tables."

Out we go. We move the tables one way and think we are finished.

Tía Blanca says, "I need you to make some changes." So back we go.

We move the tables she wants. We stand there and watch her as she looks around the room.

Thomas takes a step back and pulls my sleeve. I take a step back and he takes two more.

"Help me move these around," *Tía* Blanca says.

We do as we are told until we are done.

This time, we don't wait around. We leave *Tía* Blanca looking at the hall.

Thomas and I head out the front door.

Chapter 7

Thomas and I step into the evening. The sun is setting. The sky looks pink and orange. Kinda pretty.

We sit on the brick fence. He pulls out a vape pen, takes a puff, and hands it to me.

I look at it, put it in my mouth, and breathe in. I like the taste. It is sweet.

Thomas grabs it out of my hand and stuffs it in his pocket. *Tío* Beto is walking toward us.

"Boys, you're needed inside," he says.

We go back inside. This time we are given table-cloths to put over the tables. That takes us a while because there are so many tables.

When Thomas and I are done, we do not sneak out. *Tío* Beto gives us balloons to blow up and tie. Good thing he gives us a tank to use.

Thomas starts filling them up, then hands them to me. I try tying them, but it's too hard for me.

Thomas and I switch jobs. I fill them up and Thomas ties them. Angelica adds the string.

We stand there for what seems like hours.

The whole time, Angelica talks about school, her friends, and drama club. She is a sophomore now.

I don't know most of her friends. I don't know about drama club, either.

Drama club sounds fun.

We finally finish with the balloons.

While we were doing that, others came over and helped finish decorating. It looks nice.

We have nothing else we have to do to get ready. We just wait for everyone to get there.

Chapter 8

Thomas and I head to the kitchen. I grab two so-das for us. He grabs two beers.

He hides them in his shirt. He tells me to walk beside him. We go outside again.

This time, we don't sit on the fence. We walk to the back of the hall. It is dirty back here. Lots of trash. It even smells bad.

I want to go somewhere else, but Thomas says that we won't be found if we stay back here. I don't want to stay, but I do.

I hand him a soda. He takes both sodas. I just look at him.

He pulls out the beer bottles and opens them. He hands me one and drinks out of the other one.

I look at the beer bottle in my hand, then at him. I follow what he does.

It does not taste good. I make a face and almost spit it out. Thomas starts laughing at me.

He takes another drink, so I do too. The second time is not as bad as the first.

"Let's see who can drink it faster!" Thomas shouts.

We put the bottles to our mouths and race.

By the time we are done, I can't tell who won.

My head feels funny and so does my stomach. We throw the bottles on the ground with the rest of the trash.

We put our arms around each other and stare at the border wall. This time we see shadows around it.

We look at each other, start to laugh, and walk over to see what the shadows are.

Chapter 9

We walk through weeds and more trash. It smells really bad. I want to throw up.

I stop. Then we hear a voice say, *"La escalera."*

Thomas and I look toward the voice and see a long ladder go up against the fence. We duck and hide in the weeds.

We see a ladder and five trucks full of people. We look through the weeds and see more ladders go up.

Once the ladders are up, people start climbing them. They get to the top and put down another one. They go down the other side, then jump.

Once they are on the ground, they start running. They go all over the place.

From our hiding spot, I see the red lights and hear the sirens. It must be the border patrol. The trucks on this side take the ladders and drive away.

There is nothing else to see on this side.

I puke. Thomas pukes, too. We walk back to the hall and sneak into the bathroom.

We have to clean our shoes and our mouths.

When we are done, we go into the hall and straight to the kitchen. We need food. I eat and feel much better.

I sit by the kitchen, watching the people dance. There are a bunch of people. Some I know. Some I don't know.

"Henry, is that you?" someone asks. I turn around and see Alexia from school.

She comes over and sits by me. She starts talking about how she does not know anyone here, other than her family, and how happy she is to see me.

She asks me to dance. We have a blast.

We dance the rest of the night. She is a good dancer. She is also very pretty.

The party is over. Alexia is leaving.

She says, "See you at school, Henry."

I smile. I can't wait until Monday to see her again.

But first, I have to get through Sunday.

Chapter 10

Everyone gets up late on Sunday. It is a lazy day for us after the party. But I can't be too lazy.

I have homework to do. I open the laptop and go to Google Classroom.

I look for my assignments but can't find them. I take the laptop to my mom.

"Mom, where are my assignments?"

She looks at the screen and points to where I have to click.

I have three assignments: English, math, and science. *Great*, I think. This will take me the rest of the day.

I click on the English assignment. I have to listen to a story and answer five questions.

I listen to the story and try to answer the questions. I don't know how to answer them.

I take the laptop back to my mom and ask her for help. Before she even looks at the assignment, she asks me what the story was about.

"It's about a guy," I say.

"What did he do?" she asks.

"Stuff," I answer.

She looks at the screen and asks the first question. "Who is the main character?"

I look at her and she looks at me. I sink into the couch.

"Do you remember the name of the guy in the story?" she asks.

"Oh, oh yeah. It is . . . Gary. Yeah, that is his name," I say.

"Are you sure?" Mom asks.

I got the wrong answer.

Everyone always says that when I get it wrong. They give me another chance to get it right.

So I think, and I think some more.

"His name starts with a G, Mom, that's all I remember."

"That's OK, son. We can work with that. You know it is not Gary. Is it George, Greyson, or Greg?" she asks.

"I think it's George," I say. "No, wait, it is Greg."

"It is Greg," she says. "Now type the name in there."

Mom keeps reading the questions, and I keep giving her the wrong answers. So she gives me choices so I can pick out the right one. I really don't know the right answer, but I can see when I get the wrong one.

This takes forever. I still have math and science to do.

"Let's take a break and have something to eat," Mom says.

I know she is just as tired of my schoolwork as I am. I know she would rather do something else, but she has to help me.

I help her make some spaghetti and meatballs. Then we all have lunch together.

It's fun to sit around with my family. I like to hear them talk.

Today they talk about the party and all the things I didn't see.

They also talk about Alexia and me.

Chapter 11

We finish eating and my brother and sister get kitchen duty because I helped cook. Mom and I go back to the laptop and my homework.

I click on my math homework. It's ten multiplication and division problems.

I get my calculator from my backpack and look at the screen.

I punch in the first one: 1019/46 equals 13.5. Then I show it to mom.

Her lips tighten and she says, "Read this problem to me."

"One hundred nineteen times forty-six."

Again, she tightens her lips. I know I read it wrong.

She walks me through reading the problem and punching it into the calculator. I show her the answer and she smiles.

I clear the calculator and start punching in the next one.

She puts her hand over the calculator and says, "Do the multiplication ones first."

I look at her and breathe. "Times," I say.

"Yes, those first. Then I'll walk you through the division ones."

We get through that, and I take a bathroom break.

I sit back down and click on my science assignment. It has three parts. A reading, writing, and slide presentation.

I slam the lid down, toss it on the couch, walk into my room, and flop on the bed. I stare at the ceiling.

I can't read. I can't write. No way I can make a slide presentation.

Mom knocks on my door. She walks to my bed. She sits down and opens the laptop.

For the reading part, she starts the Google app that reads to me. I don't understand what they are talking about, but I try to listen.

When it is done, my mom goes over it with me again.

For the writing part, she turns on the microphone. I speak into it. Together, we add periods and capitals.

When we get to the slide presentation, she stops. She looks at the directions, then at me.

"We're done for tonight, son. I will go talk to the

teacher about this tomorrow."

I don't want her to go. I do want her to go. My stomach hurts.

She leaves the room and I go outside. I get my bike and go for a ride.

Chapter 12

It is Monday morning. Time to get ready for school.

My stomach hurts . . .

I hope to see Alexia.

I don't want my mom to talk to my science teacher.

Good luck to me.

I run into Alexia at the cafeteria. She invites me to eat breakfast with her.

We sit down. She says she had a lot of fun dancing with me on Saturday. I say I had fun, too. Then I don't know what else to say. I look at her and she looks at me.

I take a bite of food and she does, too. When she is done chewing, she asks me what my first class is.

I don't want to tell her, so I spill my milk. I get busy cleaning it up.

I apologize and ask her if I can walk her to class. We walk and say hi to people we both know.

I drop her off in the sixth wing and walk to the second wing. I walk slowly. I don't like for others to know where my classes are. I have classes with the dumb kids.

All except for science, PE, auto, and history. I have those classes with the regular kids.

There is one other student, Beth, who has most of my classes with me. She has PE with the girls. And science with the dumb kids. Only, Beth doesn't like it when people call them "the dumb kids."

Alexia doesn't know about the classes for dumb kids. I don't want her to know.

I walk into my classroom and see my teacher. I like his class. I like the stories we listen to and the projects we do with the stories.

We also do work that is supposed to help us learn to read better. I remember doing this kind of work since I was in fourth grade.

It didn't help me then. I don't see how it will help me now. I do it anyway.

Chapter 13

My next class is math. I stay in the same room with the same teacher. I like this class, too.

We get to use calculators and other things that make the work easier. We also do math projects.

Halfway through the class, the phone rings. Mr. Hernandez answers it. He hangs up. He pulls out a pass and fills it out.

He looks up, calls my name, and gives me the pass. He tells me to go to the counselor's office.

My stomach does something funny. I take the pass and walk to the counselor's office.

The counselor and my mom are waiting there for me. They talk about the science class I'm in and the choices I have.

I don't hear their words. All I know is that my stomach is burning.

There is silence. Mom and the counselor are looking at me.

"Son, what would you rather do? Stay in this science class or take a science class with Mr. Hernandez?"

Mr. Hernandez is my English and math teacher

already . . .

"Would I have to stay in the same room as I do for English and math?" I ask.

"Yes," says the counselor.

"Can I think about it?" I ask.

"No," Mom says. "You have to make a decision now. I can't keep coming back and missing work."

I don't say anything. I don't know what to say, really.

I know that I don't want to take science with Mr. Hernandez. I know I can't stay in the science class I'm in now.

So, I sit there and look out the window.

I hear my mom take a deep breath. "Son, if you don't decide, I will decide for you."

I look at her then look away. She decides for me and changes my science class.

Chapter 14

I don't get to leave Mr. Hernandez's room until 4th period, PE.

I love PE! It is my best class. I can do anything and everything in there right.

I walk down the breezeway to the gym. I run into Alexia. She hands me a note.

She smiles and says, "I'll see you later."

I crush the note in my hand. I feel the note getting wet. I'm sweating.

I go into the boys' bathroom and open the note. I wave it back and forth to dry it out.

I look at the words written on the paper. I can't read one of them. I don't know how she wrote them, but she doesn't write like me.

I fold the note and put it in my pocket. I bang my head against the door.

The bell rings. I run out of the bathroom to the gym. I'm late. Coach sees me and doesn't stop me.

I go into the locker room and change. I make it before they call my name.

We are playing volleyball. There are four teams. I'm the captain for one of them.

I get my team together. We warm up. We start to play.

I like to start in the server position. I serve my first ball into the net. I lose our serve. They get a point.

I'm in the back row trying to return the hits, but all I do is send them out of the court.

I call a time out and put someone in for me.

I'm out of the game. I can't play today.

I walk back and forth until it is time to change. I start walking to the locker room.

Coach calls me. He puts his hand on my shoulder and says, "Son, what's up with you today? Looks like you aren't having a good day."

"Nothing," I say.

We walk into the locker room. He goes to his office, and I go to my locker.

Chapter 15

I go to lunch next. I'm standing in line, thinking about how dumb I am.

Alexia stands next to me. "Have you read my note?" she asks.

"Not yet," I answer.

"Write back to me," she says, and walks away.

I walk away, too. I'm not hungry anymore.

I walk to my favorite tree and sit under it.

Beth sees me there. She sits next to me.

Neither of us say anything. The bell rings and we walk to history together.

In history, we sit with one of the groups of kids that needs help just like us.

It is not too bad. All of us are in groups.

For our last class, Beth and I walk to auto.

I don't understand what the teacher is saying. All I want is for this class to be over.

It finally is. I run out to my brother's car and wait.

Chapter 16

Hector drives us home. It's a quiet ride.

I get home and go straight to my room. I pull out the note.

I take a picture of it and put it into a Google document. I turn on the reading app.

The app reads it to me, but it doesn't make too much sense. It sounds like she says she likes me and wants to go to a movie.

I turn on the microphone app and talk to the computer. Then I take a piece of paper and write what the computer screen says.

I feel a little better.

Now I have a note to give to Alexia.

I don't have any homework during the week with Mr. Hernandez. Our history teacher doesn't give my class homework at all.

So I go outside and shoot some hoops until it is time to eat.

Chapter 17

We are late getting to school on Tuesday morning. Hector did not get up on time.

I run to the cafeteria. I get there. The bell rings.

Alexia gets up and starts walking. I run up to her. "Hi," I say.

She smiles.

We start walking to the sixth wing. She asks why I'm late and if I read her note. I smile at her and hand her the note I wrote.

She walks into class. I run to mine.

Not because I'm going to be tardy. Because I'm happy.

I can't wait to see Alexia at lunch time.

Chapter 18

After first period, Hector walks to the counselor's office.

He sees a group of girls. They are laughing so hard, they are crying.

"Look at this," one says.

Another girl looks at it and asks, "What does it say? It looks like it was scribbled by a second grader."

Hector slows down. He recognizes the girl holding the paper.

"I think he made a mistake when he gave that to you, don't you?" the first girl asks.

"No, he's cute but stupid."

Hector reaches in and grabs the paper. It scares the group of girls, but he doesn't care.

"Stay away from him!" he yells.

Then he turns to the girl who was holding the paper.

He can't remember her name. *Alicia, maybe?* But he doesn't really care about that, either.

He gets in her face and whispers, "If I see you talking to him again, I will make your life miserable.

So stay away from my little brother. Do you understand?"

The girl nods and walks away. Her friends go
with her.

Hector looks at the note.

i lik u to lettuce gone the moving fiday
Henry.

Hector folds the note. He puts it in his pocket. He
puts his head on the wall.

He hears the bell ring. He turns arounds and
goes back to class.

He forgot what he needed the counselor for. All
he can think about is Henry.

Chapter 19

At lunchtime, Hector sees Henry in the cafeteria. He walks over and tells him he got Henry's lunch.

Then Hector invites him to sit with the basketball team. Henry looks at his brother.

He asks, "Is this a joke?"

Hector puts his arm around him. Together, they join the basketball team.

They talk about games. They talk about basketball. They talk about trips.

Then lunchtime is over.

The team leaves the lunchroom. Henry stays behind.

He looks around. He looks for Alexia. He sees her.

He starts walking toward her, then stops.

A boy comes up to her. He puts his arm around her and they walk away.

For the second time that hour, Henry is shocked. First his brother and the basketball team. Now Alexia.

Henry is very confused. He catches up with Beth. They walk to class together in silence.

Chapter 20

That night after everyone is in bed, Hector knocks on his mother's bedroom door. He walks in and sits on his father's side of the bed.

He hands the paper over. Then he lies down and covers his face with his arm.

His mom takes the paper. She opens it up and reads.

Hector hears her sniffling. He uncovers his face and sees her crying.

Hector tells her how he got the note. He tells her what he said to the girls.

His mom breathes in and looks away. "Thank you for looking out for your brother," she says. "It's not your responsibility. That belongs to your father and me. Know that we appreciate it."

"Will he always need someone to look out for him?"

"Yes, he will. He does not learn like you do. He will always need help with reading, writing, and math."

Hector nods.

It may be his parents' responsibility, but it's his,

too.

Chapter 21

On Wednesday morning, Hector and Henry drive to school.

On their way, they stop by Beth's house. They take her to school, too.

The three of them walk into the school together and head to the cafeteria. They get their food and sneak out to Henry and Beth's tree.

Hector stays and has breakfast with them.

Beth and Henry head to class together. But Beth is not quiet today.

She tells Henry about her dog, Nick. Henry laughs at her story.

He looks around. He is looking for Alexia, but he doesn't see her.

Beth tells another story. It makes Henry laugh.

Together, they go into class to start their day.

About the Author

Mari Sexton is an elementary school teacher who was drawn to special education because a child with a learning disability touched their heart.

About the Publisher

Storyshares is a publisher focused on supporting the millions of teens and adults who struggle with reading by creating a new shelf in the library specifically for them. The ever-growing collection features content that is compelling and culturally relevant for teens and adults, yet still readable at a range of lower reading levels.

Storyshares generates content by engaging deeply with writers, bringing together a community to create this new kind of book. With more intrigu- ing and approachable stories to choose from, the teens and adults who have fallen behind are improving their skills and beginning to discover the joy of reading. or more information, visit storyshares.org.

Easy to Read. Hard to put down.

www.ingramcontent.com/pod-product-compliance
Lightning Source LLC
Chambersburg PA
CBHW071226170626
46809CB00005BA/1961